TROUBLE IN LIFE

RAJVEER SINGH

ISBN 979-888546133-7

Dedicated To all Females Gender who face different kinds of problems in their Life..

Dedictated To One Who Is Reading This With Their Eyes!!!

Contents

Foreword

To The Reader Of This Book

In Submitting of Problems Faced by females in thier Life is manscripted in Book form , I believe That Few Words Relatively gonna express what is book about..

I and My Friend Mr.Luv Singh has expressed our feeling in way that u gonna relate the problems Females faces In Their Lifeee...

Luv Singh Is Illustrator Of Book , Basically punjabi Singer who lives In Belgium But from Punjab{India}.. He Loves Boxing When He Free and He Likes To write Songs that make listener feel good..

Rajveer Singh , Writer Of "Trouble In Life" .. He is Punjabi Songwriter Who made his debut with song " Hold ME " and Free time he likes to write something for problems which are ignored by society..

Preface

We all faced Different kinds of problems in our life in every second .It could be like money shortage, love problems, family problems, and society mentality for individuals, religions issues, and many more till the least...

Some huge problems or Worst Problems , especially Female faces is sexually harassment , rape , dowry related domestic violence , safety concerns and body shaming and Acid attack and many more..

Did you think Problems Ends Here?

Nopes!!

I am here to share my thoughts in fiction or with Some imaginary stories that can easily relate youu with issues. Yeah I have never faced All Kind Problems but Tried to Feel it, I gonna say, which you are unaware off or You Knew but You didn't care for that...

Acknowledgements

I have to start by thanking my awesome Friends, Aakriti Jain . From reading early drafts to giving me advice on the cover to keeping the munchkins out of my hair so I could edit, she was as important to this book getting done as I was. Thank you so much, Yaar." Being specific in thanks is all about making them feel special Posts that made my mind to write something in book form..

Writing a book is harder than I thought and more rewarding than I could have ever imagined. None of this would have been possible without my best friend, Sakshi Singh. She was the first friend I made when I was in standard 8 who helped me in every bad part of life . She stood by me during every struggle and all my successes. That is true friendship.

I'm eternally grateful to my brother Premdeep Singh, who took in an extra mouth to feed when he didn't have to. He taught me discipline, tough love, manners, respect, and so much more that has helped me succeed in life. I truly have no idea where I'd be if he hadn't given me best way when I was Confused in my life or became the father figure whom I desperately needed at that age.

To my family. To My loving mom: for always being the person I could turn to during those dark and desperate years. She sustained me in ways that I never knew that I needed. To my cousin brother Ranjay, and sisters, Riya and Rashi: thank you for letting me know that you had nothing but great memories of me. So thankful to have you back in my life.

Finally, to all those who have been a part of my getting there: Bhanu Pratap Singh, Amandeep Singh {Inquistive},

Tegi Pannu, Chiranjeevi Prasad, Vaibhav, and Brother Bhanu (RIP). Luv Singh , Simar panag , Omika Jain, Dr.Prabhjot kaur , G.Sidhu and Anurag kumar, Shushant kashi ....

Prologue

Life Is Like A Movie!

Problems are Like A Barriers ;

''Keep Fighting' , ''Keep Winning'' !!

CHAPTER ONE

GIRL CHILD ABUSE

Firstly, While most People thinks of larger problems like rape, harassment , body shaming , safety concerns and denial of education to girl children in rural Areas. I want to address this Question from an average woman that Grew Comfortably in India as Child. We all Listen Some Family Never Wants A girl child, if they are born then their addressed like burden and Liability. I guess No one treat a girl child is gift.

I want to remind you that Girl child is always gift for family except of boys, You Know Why?The girl Child Always Think of their family Respect before Doing Anything but Boys never think of their respect how can they can think about their family respect.

I can Give An Example , In Every Rape news, Female gender Try to Keep Silent As Its can Harm her Family Respect In society but culprit never Feels Shame or Have Fear Of Losing his Family respect.

Body Shaming

By Some estimates, 94% of teenage girls In India have been shamed for the way their bodies look and their dress. Yes, that means nearly every women experienced body shaming before she heads to college , walking to streets or public places or driving a vehicle. The shame many woman experienced throughout their lives can have lasting and potentially debilitating effects on their self-esteem. As a result, only 4% of women consider themselves to be beautiful and safe.

That's really heartbreaking.

While many people point their fingers at social media and the media at large, body shaming has been around since the beginning of time, today there are simple more opportunities. The story below speaks for them and I am sure that you will get bit of yourself in each of them.

"Aye moti , Aye Kali , Aye kali "These are some common nicknames which are actually quite insulting. Isha used to be a fat and short kid so the people around her pretty much addressed as Moti or Nati when she was 14 year old. She used to hate it as it made her feel inferior. Why didn't these people Call her

genius,smart or Artistic?

She always did well at school and was great at dance. Whenever she went, easily made friend. What really defined her – the way she looked or the person she was?

Often People don't realize that calling someone mean nicknames related to their body or skin color is not only racist but also provokes negative emotions in that person. She tried to ignore these comments but how can one ignore cousins and family?

This Subtitle form of bullying made her so angry. For a long time, She ignored looking at the mirror till she realized that

{Accept how you are, what personality or interest and quality you have. Don't bother what people say because it's their work. They feel sad when you are happy in your life, they can be mostly nearest person [family, friend and neighbors] just live the life.}

So she challenized her anger into making herself better at the things that she enjoyed, the things that were the real her. She joined martial arts, dancing, and music and wrote short poems. She grades were always best. Without any reference, She managed to find a job at places which which had a great work atmosphere. The People who called her names continued to do so but her confidence in herself was enough to let these people get into her mind and hurt her. Her husband is great human being. Ever since she got married, he has loved her for the real one. This is what they must strive for, to be original and creative.

The Real one is not the way she looks but the way she conduct herself. Her qualities, honesty, simplicity make her proud. She may be fat or short but she never complains for that except she has great sense of humor. Sometimes stress of motherhood upsets her moods yet she does her best every day. So what if she get failures? These fears have taught her to believe on herself. She lost many friends on this journey but she has no regrets because she could win and was best in her relationships. The Scars on her body and the grey hair are proof of the hard work she has done so far. Her anger, frustration, and fears are as much a part of me as is her *loving self. This for her...*

"She never complain the god why he made her like this, she faces many troubles in her life's but she never diverted back ... She fought back and won the life troubles which never ends in any period "

So I suggest you be confident and happy as you are, never tried to change yourself for anyone or any comments.

This was first impassive story that can easily relate you to problems of body shaming in Female's life. Yes Isha Is an Imaginary character. So try to be Isha who win and ignored from this problems.

CHAPTER TWO

DRESS SHAMING

We All Know about the Problem body shaming but it also have dearest friend known as 'Dress Shaming'

It also Gives birth for different kind of problems in girl's life...

When it comes to what women wear, the entire world has an opinion to offer but nothing is more demoralizing than other women dress shame you. Every woman in this world has the right to wear what she wants to. She isn't answerable to anyone on her choice of clothes. But often it is women who take it upon themselves to police other women's clothes on the grounds of morality, fashion or even body size. Doesn't this entirely defeat the purpose of our cry for liberation from dress policing?

Pointing Someone for what she/they wear!!

Here in India, we as a society, have a tendency to jump to quick and very vocal judgments in the name of propriety. Without a doubt, one area where this has been painfully obvious for decades is the public shaming of women who wear revealing clothes. Of course, this is really a worldwide issue, and more than likely, if you're a woman, you've encountered the effects of these judgments personally. Whetheryou've been told by a parent that you simply won't be allowed out of the house in a skirt that short, reprimanded by an educator or leader in your religious community for being too suggestive in your apparel choices, or informed by a heckler that your clothing is making them feel a certain way, you know the sting of implications made about your personal worth based upon how you've chosen to explore fashion.

What's truly unfortunate is that while many people operate from and hide behind the guise of being helpful or protective, they fail to recognize that, for men and women alike, fashion is a form of self-expression, and just as an artist's style grows and adapts over many years, so does our sense of personal style. The clothing that we wear is, in many ways, a projection of what we are going through emotionally and mentally at a given time, and while helping your daughter/sister/friend/ mother understand that her self-worth goes far beyond her sexual appeal is hugely beneficial, being overly critical of her self-exploration is not. While we all want to support current and future generations of women in making wise choices based upon their innate value as human beings, not from a place of being sexually objectified, it's important to keep in mind that they/we are navigating an entirely unique world climate, facing new social norms, and pioneering (hopefully) more progressive ways of thinking.

Recently, I found myself sincerely concerned with a post made by friend on Instagram[@aakritijain]. It was another reminder of how our society still subconsciously considers harshly judging others to be a worthwhile pastime. We continue to think it acceptable or helpful even to publicly (in person or via social media) shame women for wearing too little or too much, and a myriad of other offenses. And in an effort to encourage the wellbeing of all women, I'd like to take a few moments to point out why doing so is both wildly inappropriate (even more than what you may perceive a woman's fashion choice to be), and can be detrimental to society as a whole.

CHAPTER THREE

Destroying Confidence Instead Of Fostering Positive Self Image

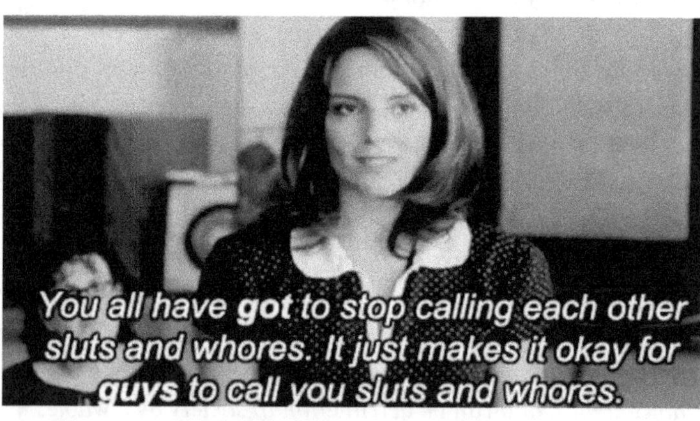

Before you turn to your daughter and tell her you refuse to see her dress like such a slut (I know, harsh, but tons of parents do or threaten to without even thinking), please remember that there are damaging effects to having one's personal appearance harshly criticized. Especially when it's your sexual

appearance that's being called into question. Teenage girls have the already difficult task of navigating their emerging sexual desires in a society that doesn't always teach sexual education or embrace the reality that women can be intelligent, respectable, and sexually alluring people. What they need most from their parents is emotional support and constructive guidelines that will help them find their own sense of style while building a level of discernment around when certain self-expression serves those best, and when it can hinder them.

It's also important that we encourage young women to examine why they are inclined to be concerned about the appearance or behavior of another woman or girl. Slut-shaming is disparaging and harmful, has psychological repercussions, and sadly can lead to tragic outcomes. And although many men and women think that discouraging a woman from wearing clothing that show's too much of her body is positive, the effects can be quite confusing, especially if she views her body as beautiful, strong, and considers highlighting those physical attributes an intrinsic part of her identity. Remember, we're born in the buff, so the line between too much and just enough can be pretty vague when it comes to covering skin that doesn't initially come covered anyway.

CHAPTER FOUR

Perpetuating the Fallacy of Attention-Seeking.

Across the Internet and in various social circles you'll hear proponents of modesty claiming that women who wear skin-baring outfits are attention seekers. All of us. Period. That is an unfortunate and all too erroneous casual oversimplification. Women choose their wardrobe based off of varying factors, including but not limited to: functionality, mobility, comfort, pattern, fabric, visual appeal (in the form of cut, style, and appearance on one's body), trends, emotional state, mental state, sexual appetite, and iconic influence. All of these aspects are okay; because they are all facets of who we are has humans. To assume Girls are walking around in short shorts because they are seeking your attention is absolutely absurd. If someone wear short shorts in spite of external attention, because she enjoy the feeling of sunshine on her legs and the flexibility that they afford her in active lifestyle. I don't appreciate the prying eyes,

Enter Caption

Do not do a woman the injustice of projecting what you'd like to think she's thinking upon her. Better yet, do not assume you can read the mind of anyone, because unless your telepathy game is genuinely strong, you're probably mistaken...

CHAPTER FIVE

RAPE CULTURE

If you have any doubts about how prevalent rape is in our culture, according to a study conducted by the Center for Disease Control and Prevention, here in the India, nearly one in five women say they've been sexually assaulted. But almost more frightening than that statistic is the approach our society tends to default to in terms of why a woman has been raped. Too many people throw around terrible phrases like "She was asking for it" or suggest that what a woman was wearing either implied that she wanted the sexual activity so it was okay, or that the coverage of her clothing or its cut caused her rapist to lose control.

This is a huge issue and one of great concern. A woman's attire may be a reflection of her mood, however, in no circumstance does an outfit signify a woman's consent to sexual activity. Nor does it signify an invitation. It is our responsibility as individuals to recognize personal boundaries and to respect each other's wishes when it comes to our bodies and sexuality. Self-control is paramount, and the way to prevent continued rape culture is to teach self-control and respect for all sexes beginning at a young age. It also means teaching the difference between what we see in porn and what we see in real life.

Continuing to limit the clothing options for girls and women and categorizing certain items as being too distracting only does society, women, and men a disservice. It teaches us to believe that our bodies are somehow shameful, and that showing our shape will lead to pain, suffering, and dehumanization, when instead we should be teaching young boys and men that a woman's body is her business and no different than a man's body in terms of worth..

SHAMING SEXUALITY

Along with shaming women on the basis of physical appearance comes the implication that somehow women should not be sexually active or enjoy healthy sexual relationships. The good news is we no longer live in a society where a woman's virtue is based off of her virginity. The bad news is some people still act like we do. And they make assumptions about a woman's sexual life based off of the clothes she is wearing on a given day.

Don't be shamed of your Sexuality

When it comes right down to it, plenty of women who have never had sex wear clothes that show their chests, their thighs, their shoulders, ankles, and collar bones. Conversely, many women who have had lots of sex don't like to show off their bodies at all and not because they feel any shame in it. The simple truth is that most often, when a woman wears clothing that shows the curves of her body or reveals her skin, it is because she likes the way she looks, and feels good in the the outfit. We need not overcomplicate her motives. She may be trying on a new style, she may be on her way to see her fiancé who has been overseas for six months, or she may simply be enjoying the warmth of the sun on her skin.

*Regardless of the motivation behind why a woman is wearing yoga pants (because they're insanely comfortable!) or a short skirt (because her legs are her favorite body part, and it makes her happy to see them), we need to remember that women have the right to explore and express their sexuality. To suggest otherwise implies that we consider them inferior and unworthy of enjoying basic human experiences, and that, my friends, is simply inconceivable***and unacceptable..***

Lets Have Story Of Akashi To relate this problem[This problem cannot be defined with one girl story]

The first time Akashi got in trouble for clothing at school, or got "dress-coded," she was 12.It was around the time that wearing leggings and jean skirts was super "in." That day she wore a jean skirt, likely an inch shorter than school allowed, black leggings to cover up the rest of my legs so she would not get in trouble, and a scoop-neck T-shirt.

She was in science class working on a group project. She felt a tap on my shoulder from her homeroom teacher, who had seen me earlier that day. She asked if she could speak with her outside and she obliged. She then told her something that has stuck with her: "Akashi, I know you like fashion, but I have heard some boys in your class talking about the way you are dressed. I think it would be best if you go change." I was ashamed. She felt ashamed that people were talking about her clothing. She felt ashamed of her outfit choice. And most of all, She felt ashamed of my body.

At the time, she felt as if she had done something wrong, but in retrospect she was the one who had been wronged. Fervent dress-coding is not only sexist; it also reinforces an already-prevalent body shaming culture, kick-starting the phenomenon at an early age. I understand that she /someone cannot expect to be able to wear crop tops and ripped jeans in the fourth grade, but school dress codes create an environment where women learn early on to feel ashamed of their bodies.

Women have dress codes enforcing how much of their legs they can show, how much of their chest they can show, how much of their stomachs they can show, and even how much of their shoulders they can show. Telling a young girl that she cannot wear a tank top with 1-inch straps is really telling her that even her shoulders are not acceptable for public display.

Telling a young girl that she cannot wear shorts or skirts that do not reach her knees tells her that she doesn't dictate what is appropriate about her body society does. Telling a young girl that she cannot show her chest tells her that if her body distracts men it is her fault, not theirs. Telling any woman anything about their bodies fosters body shaming.

The day she got dress-coded, she felt badly about my body, and she knows that she is not the first. She was humiliated just for being herself and celebrating her body. Being told every day that she couldn't wear certain things framed how she feels about my body.

Although she now have few qualms about wearing lower-cut shirts and tighter skirts, every once in a while she do feel indecent or ashamed about showing her body. This is not fair.

Dress code guidelines, as they are now, are unacceptable. We must fight for right to own bodies, and stop telling young girls how to feel about theirs.

CHAPTER SEVEN

Rejection Hurts!!

When your partner feels you have rejected them, whether their feeling is fair or not, you are at risk of your partner lashing out in anger and aggression, potentially with violence.

NOOOO!!

One more woman died last Year because she dared to say 'no' to a man who was not used to handling rejection...In Haryana, a 20-year-old student was shot and killed outside her college by a man whose overtures for 'friendship' had been rejected by the girl. The chilling incident was caught on CCTV camera.

TWO horrifying episodes- all in one month are reported from different parts of the country. Many more have likely gone unreported and unrecorded. These are not merely isolated instances of crimes against women, they are about a sense of sexual entitlement, a culture of toxic masculinity, nurtured, protected and normalised by patriarchal belief systems that allow men to think it is their right to silence and annihilate women who dare to refuse their 'love'.

From being sexually assaulted, doused with acid, to being set on fire, 'rejection violence' -- where women face the consequences for saying 'no' to men has become a revoltingly familiar phenomenon in India .

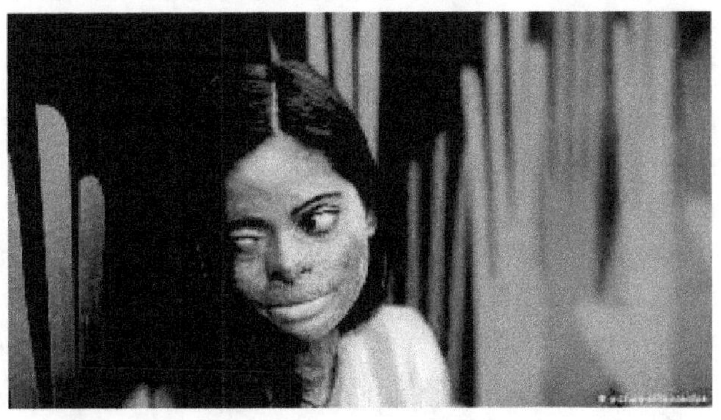

Acid Attacks Victim !!

We have time and again expressed our outrage against such violence, sought to bring in stricter legislations and rallied for better support mechanisms for survivors of such violence. Yet, women continue to be subjected to violence with impunity for asserting their right to say 'NO'..

It is a form of dehumanisation of women -- a refusal to consider women as equal human beings with the right to make their own choices. Women's rejection is viewed not only as an insult to the male ego but as an indefemsible attack on the very essence of being a 'REAL MARD'. The notions of control and domination are integral to such constructions of masculinity while women are excepted to the docile , pliant and submissive . Any transgressions from these unsaid/unwritten but deep rooted norms warrant violence ..

India is one of 36 countries in the world where it is legal for a husband to rape his wife. Forcing sexual intercourse on a woman against her will the inability to accept her right to say 'no' ..When legitimised by legal systems, not only reinforces and sanctions a violent and toxic masculinity where women are mere 'property' of men, but actively encourages it. The often-cited argument for refusing to criminalise marital rape is that it will destabilise the sanctity of marriage. Does not rape itself destabilise the sanctity of marriage?

It is quite ironic that while we are increasingly invested in 'saving' women from falling in love with the 'wrong' man (read 'Love Jihad'), we are quite accepting of a culture that allows men to express their 'love' in violent ways. It is high time that we channelised our 'collective conscience' and energies away from treating women as mere pawns in male-dominated social institutions, controlling and dictating their agency and choices..

Instead, we must focus on educating our current and future generations not to define their self-worth by artificial and unrealistic standards of masculinity and femininity.Strengthening our legal/judicial processes is imperative, but at the same time we must recognise, call out and challenge everyday sexism and misogyny in public as well as private spaces that sustain and encourage regressive

gender norms thereby legitimising violence.

1984 Sikh Genocide

Crimes never see age i.e Rape victims !!

Genocides may vary in magnitude and scale but one thing that remains common is the vulnerability of women and children to sexual violence and 1984 Sikh genocide was no different on that. **1984 India's secret guilty a book by Pav Singh** *pour some light on Mass rapes that were committed by organized killers in an organized manner with intent to humiliate and demoralize, which were either ignored due to the social stigma attached to it or wereefficiently suppressed by state machinery due to national shame. Testimonies from survivors speak unimaginable horrors, women and girl children were stripped and gang-raped while their husbands and sons were forced to watch.One testimony from a forty-five-year-old woman describes that horror, On Nov 1, a group of teenagers no older than fourteen or fifteen entered their house murdered her husband and gang-raped her in front of her son and later her son was burnt alive by sprinkling kerosene on it and setting him on fire..*

Massive Rape and Sexual Victims!!

Simply I wanna Say Indian Congress [followers and lover of Indira Gandhi} set/made world Massive rape records in history which will be unforgettable .[DECEMBER 1984]

They are more Stories and facts Of massive 1984 rapes but I didn't want to share it because itz quite horrible and painful for anyone who going to read or listen about it...

Ending But Not Least

Lets join Hand Together and Stand For Females Who could be your mother, sister and More..

STOP CRIMES AGAINST FEMALES

STOP RAPE CULTURES

STOP DOMESTIC VIOLENCE

STOP BODY SHAMING

STOP DRESS SHAMING

STOP SAYING SLUTS

STOP ACID ATTACKs

STOP HUMAN TRAFFICING AND FORCED PROSTITUTION

STOP SEXUAL ASSAULTS

www.ingramcontent.com/pod-product-compliance
Lightning Source LLC
Chambersburg PA
CBHW060921130726
48001CB00006B/2354